NICK

SpongeBob SquarePants

UFO!

by Adam Beechen   illustrated by Zina Saunders

SCHOLASTIC INC.
New York Toronto London Auckland Sydney
Mexico City New Delhi Hong Kong Buenos Aires

"Grow, flower, grow!
Grow, flower, grow!"
SpongeBob and his best friend,
Patrick, sang as they marched
through SpongeBob's garden.

"What are you two
weirdos doing?"
Squidward asked.

"If you talk to plants,
   they grow fast," Patrick told him.
"And if we sing to my daffodils,
   they should grow even faster!"
   SpongeBob added.

Squidward was about to tell them
to be quiet, when suddenly . . .

something very big blocked
out the light from above!

Everyone in Bikini Bottom met
to talk about what had happened.
They decided aliens must be
invading Bikini Bottom.

"We should run and hide!"
someone shouted.
"No, we should hide and then run!"
someone shouted back.

Patrick got scared and ran around
in circles.
"I do not know whether to run or
hide!" he cried.

Squidward headed to his house.
"I do not think it's the
end of the world," he grumbled.
"Everyone should go home and stop
making so much noise!"

"Maybe this is not the end
of the world," Sandy suggested.
"Maybe it's just something we do
not understand yet."

"If Sandy is not scared,
then neither am I,"
SpongeBob said.

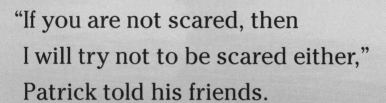

"If you are not scared, then
    I will try not to be scared either,"
    Patrick told his friends.
"Well, we are scared,"
    everyone else said.
"And we are going to
    run and hide!"

"What are we going to do?"
SpongeBob asked.
"I think we should find out
what is making that shadow,"
Sandy told him.

"We can use my rocket ship
to take us to the Outer Waters
so we can get a closer look,"
Sandy said.

The friends gathered everything
they would need for their trip.
"Why do we need sandwiches?"
Sandy asked Patrick.
"Rockets make me hungry,"
Patrick explained.

They climbed into the rocket ship.
"Buckle up, fellas. It is going
to be a bumpy ride!" Sandy shouted
as they blasted off.

Patrick buckled in his sandwiches.

They saw all sorts of creatures
they had never seen before.
Patrick was a little scared,
but he tried to be brave
like SpongeBob and Sandy.

Back in his house in Bikini Bottom,
Squidward suddenly realized
how quiet it was outside.
He had not been scared of the
shadow before, but he was now.

Suddenly there was a loud knock
at his door!

"Squidward!" Mrs. Puff shouted
from the other side of the door.
"Are you sure you do not want
to come hide with us?"

"No," Squidward yelled back.
"I am not scared! I am busy playing
my clarinet!"
He tried to play his clarinet,
but he was so scared, it sounded
even worse than usual!

When Mrs. Puff and Mr. Krabs left,
Squidward quickly hid under his bed.
"I am not letting the end of the world
get me . . . or my clarinet!" he said.

Sandy's rocket soared closer
and closer to the shadow.
Patrick became more and more scared.
He could not help it.

"What if that shadow really is the
end of the world?" Patrick asked.
"Then at least we will have seen it
up close," SpongeBob answered.
"And we will have seen it together,"
Sandy agreed.

Finally, they were close enough
to see what was making the shadow—
and they could not believe it!

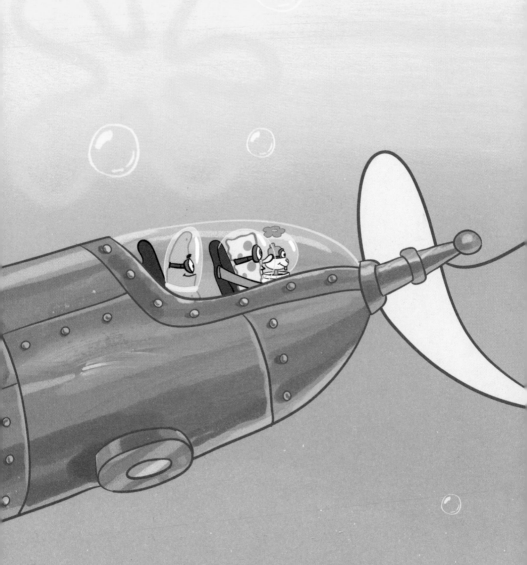

"Hey, guys," said their old friend
   Stan the manta.
"I am back from school
   to visit Bikini Bottom!"
"Wow! You got big," Sandy gasped.

"Why are you up here blocking all
   the light?" Sandy asked. "You really
   spooked everybody!"
"I am sorry," Stan told them.
"I could not remember
   where I used to live."

"We will show you the way,"
SpongeBob said.
"Everyone will be happy to see you!"
"Especially since you are not
the end of the world," Patrick said.
No one was happier than he was!

Everyone was very happy to see Stan
again. They celebrated by playing
a new game Patrick made up called
run-and-hide-and-seek.

Squidward did not play along.
If he had played, he would have won.
He stayed in his hiding place
for two weeks!